My 1ST GRAPHIC NOVEL

TRAIN TRIP

My First Graphic Novels are published by Stone Arch Books
A Capstone Imprint
151 Good Counsel Drive, P.O. Box 669
Mankato, Minnesota 56002
*www.capstonepub.com*

*Library of Congress Cataloging-in-Publication Data*
Meister, Cari.
    Train trip / by Cari Meister ; illustrated by Marilyn Janovitz.
    p. cm. — (My first graphic novel)
    ISBN 978-1-4342-1616-8 (library binding)
    ISBN 978-1-4342-2289-3 (softcover)
    1. Graphic novels. [1. Graphic novels. 2. Railroad trains—Fiction.] I. Janovitz, Marilyn, ill.
II. Title.
PZ7.7.M45Tr 2010
741.5'973—dc22

                                                              2008053374


Summary: Hannah and Will take their first train trip.


Creative Director: Heather Kindseth
Graphic Designer: Emily Harris

Printed in the United States of America in Melrose Park, Illinois.
092009
005620LKS10

My 1ST GRAPHIC NOVEL

# TRAIN TRIP

by Cari Meister
illustrated by Marilyn Janovitz

STONE ARCH BOOKS
MINNEAPOLIS   SAN DIEGO

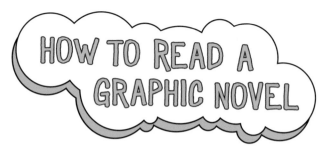

# HOW TO READ A GRAPHIC NOVEL

Graphic novels are easy to read. Boxes called panels show you how to follow the story. Look at the panels from left to right and top to bottom.

Read the word boxes and word balloons from left to right as well. Don't forget the sound and action words in the pictures.

The pictures and the words work together to tell the whole story.

Hannah and Will are going to the museum.

The museum is in another city.

They will take the train. Will checks the train times.

# The train station is busy.

Some people are reading.

Some people are eating.

People are buying tickets.

Trains come.

Trains go.

Hannah and Will find track four.

The tracks rumble. The train is here!

The doors open. People rush out.

People rush in.

Hannah and Will sit by the window.

The doors slide shut.

The ticket taker collects tickets.

Hannah cannot find her ticket.

She looks in her pocket.
It is not there.

She looks in her backpack.
It is not there.

She looks in her shoe.

Dark clouds fill the sky.
It starts to rain.

The drops hit the windows. The
rain makes everything look blurry.

The rain doesn't last long. The sun peeks out again.

The train goes over a bridge.
Hannah closes her eyes.

The train goes through a tunnel.
Hannah closes her eyes.

The train rattles by the first station.

The train rushes by
the second station.

Hannah checks her watch.

The train screeches to a stop.
The doors slide open.

Hannah and Will get up from their seats. What a great trip!

The End

# ABOUT THE AUTHOR

Cari Meister is the author of many books for children, including the My Pony Will series and *Luther's Halloween*. She lives on a small farm in Minnesota with her husband, four sons, three horses, one dog, and one cat. Cari enjoys running, snowshoeing, horseback riding, and yoga. She loves to visit libraries and schools.

# ABOUT THE ILLUSTRATOR

Marilyn Janovitz has written and illustrated numerous books for children. Many of her books have been translated into several languages. Marilyn's work has also been used in advertising, editorial, and textile design. Marilyn works in her closet-sized studio, where she can look out and see the Empire State Building twenty blocks away.

# GLOSSARY

**museum** (myoo-ZEE-uhm)—a place where art, science, and history objects are displayed

**station** (STAY-shuhn)—a place where passengers are let on and off a train

**ticket** (TIK-it)—a piece of paper that shows that you paid to ride a train

**track** (TRAK)—a rail for a train to run on

# DISCUSSION QUESTIONS

1.) Hannah and Will are going to a museum. Have you been to a museum? If so, what did you see there?

2.) Hannah was scared when the train was on the bridge. What makes you scared? What do you do when you are scared?

3.) Imagine that you work for the train company. How would you get people to take the train instead of taking a car?

# WRITING PROMPTS

1.) Hannah and Will are going to a museum to see mummies. Draw a picture of a mummy and a mummy case. Be sure to name your mummy.

2) Draw a map of Hannah and Will's trip on the train. Make sure to include the bridge and the tunnel.

3.) Throughout the book, there are sound and action words next to some of the picture. Pick at least two of those words. Then write your own sentences using those words.

# THE 1ST STEP INTO GRAPHIC NOVELS

These books are the perfect introduction to graphic novels. Combine an entertaining story with comic book panels, exciting action elements, and bright colors, and a safe graphic novel is born.

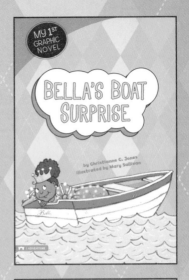

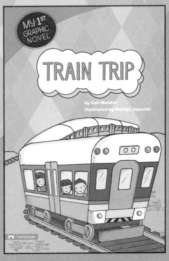

# WAIT!

## DON'T CLOSE THE BOOK!

# THERE'S MORE!

## FIND MORE:

Games & Puzzles
Heroes & Villains
Authors & Illustrators

AT...

# www.CAPSTONEKIDS.com

STILL WANT MORE?